CHRISTMAS FOR 10

by
Cathryn Falwell

Clarion Books/New York

Clarion Books
a Houghton Mifflin Company imprint
215 Park Avenue South, New York, NY 10003
Copyright © 1998 by Cathryn Falwell

The illustrations are collages made from cut paper
and fabric, with watercolor detail.
The text was set in 30-point Granjon.

www.houghtonmifflinbooks.com

Printed in Singapore

Library of Congress Cataloging-in-Publication Data
Falwell, Cathryn.
Christmas for 10 / by Cathryn Falwell.
p.   cm.
Summary: Rhyming text presents a traditional Christmas celebration
in which various objects and people are counted.
ISBN 0-395-85581-0   PA ISBN 0-618-37836-7
[1. Christmas—Fiction. 2. Counting. 3. Stories in rhyme.]
I. Title.
PZ8.3.F2163Ch   1998
[E]—dc21   97-46134
CIP
AC

TWP   10 9 8 7 6 5 4 3

For my dad,
Warren David Falwell,
for making Christmas magical

1 one
star
for the top
of the
Christmas
tree

2 two
angels
with wings

3 three royal kings

4 four
children play
in harmony

 five
snuggle
up near

six
stories
to hear

7 seven
tasty
candy canes

8 eight
reindeer
that fly

9 nine
ribbons
to tie

10 ten
hands
string the
popcorn
chains

1 one
wreath
welcomes
guests
to the door

2 two
will make

3 three
will bake

4 four
will taste
and ask
for more

5 five
baskets
to pack

6 six
presents
to stack

7 seven
bright
candles
standing tall

eight
voices sing

nine
silver bells
ring

10 ten
joyful
folks
wish
peace
for
all!